C. mathiesen

DO PIGS SIT

Zelasney

AUTHOR

Do Pigs Sit In Tree?

TITLE

DATE DUE	BORROWER	

DO PIGS SIT
IN TREES?

Jean Zelasney

Illustrated by Mr. Stobbs

MODERN CURRICULUM PRESS
Cleveland • Toronto

Library of Congress Cataloging in Publication Data

Zelasney, Jean.
 Do pigs sit in trees?

 Summary: A young pig in search of his mother thinks of all the things she likes to do and tracks her down.
 [1. Pigs—Fiction. 2. Animals—Fiction. 3. Mothers—Fiction] I. Sumichrast, Józef. II. Title.
PZ7.Z396Do   [E]   81–4070
ISBN 0-8136-5615-X Library Edition
ISBN 0-8136-5115-8 Paper Edition

      5   6   7   8   9   10   89 88 87

Quentin the pig went into his house. He was tired and hungry from a long walk.

"Is dinner ready?" asked Quentin, but no one answered him.

Quentin looked around the quiet house. I wonder where everyone is, he thought. Dinner should be ready.

He looked again in all the rooms, but no one was there.

"Where's my mother?" asked Quentin. "Where are my brothers? They're always home by this time. Maybe everyone is lost, and I'd better find them."

So Quentin went to find his lost family.

Quentin looked inside the barn, but no one was there. He looked behind the tractor, but no one was there.

Quentin saw the ducks looking for bugs in the grass. Quentin asked them if they had seen his mother.

"No, we haven't," said one of the ducks, "but have you looked in the pond? When our mother is missing, we find her there. She likes to swim in the deep water and walk in the mud. Maybe your mother is there."

Quentin thought. Would his mother like to swim in a pond? He pictured her in his mind.

"My mother can't be there," said
Quentin. "She likes mud, but she doesn't
like to swim."

Quentin started looking again. He followed the path to the chicken house.

Quentin asked the baby chicks, "Have you seen my mother? She's lost, and it's time for my dinner."

"No," said a little chick, "but have you looked in our nests? Our mother likes to lay eggs there after she digs in the dirt. Maybe your mother is there."

Quentin thought. Would his mother be in a nest? He pictured her in his mind.

"My mother can't be in a nest," said Quentin. "She likes to dig in the dirt, but she never lays eggs in a nest."

Quentin didn't know where to go next, and he was getting so hungry it was hard to think.

Then a robin landed on the ground. The robin asked Quentin how he was.

"I'm scared," said Quentin, and a big tear rolled down his nose. "Mother is lost. It's past time for my dinner, and I have to find her."

"My mother is easy to find," said the robin. "All I do is check the trees. Mother sits in a tree right behind the farmhouse and watches the farmer's wife clean the corn. Maybe your mother is there."

Quentin thought. Would his mother sit in a tree? He pictured her in his mind.

"She can't be in a tree," said Quentin. "She likes corn, but she never sits in a tree."

19

Then Quentin sat down to think. He had to find his mother. He knew she wouldn't be swimming. She wouldn't be sitting in a nest. She would never sit in a tree. Mother did not do those things.

Then Quentin had an idea. "I'll think of all the things Mother likes to do," he said.

He remembered that his mother liked mud, that she liked to dig in dirt, and that she liked corn. Now all he had to do was to think of a place with all three of those things.

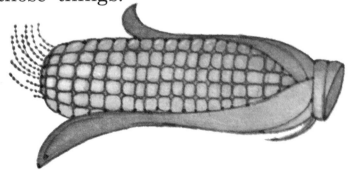

Quentin thought of the cornfield. It had dirt, it had corn, and it even had mud by the pond at one end of the field.

Quentin ran to the cornfield as fast as he could go.

Quentin was right. There were his mother and brothers in the field.

Quentin was so happy that he gave each of them a hug. Then he told his mother how he had tracked her down, and Quentin's mother told him how smart he was.

Quentin asked, "Why weren't you at home? I looked all over for you."

Quentin's mother said, "Did you forget? You said that you would meet us here for dinner. We had corn for dinner, and there's plenty of corn left for you."

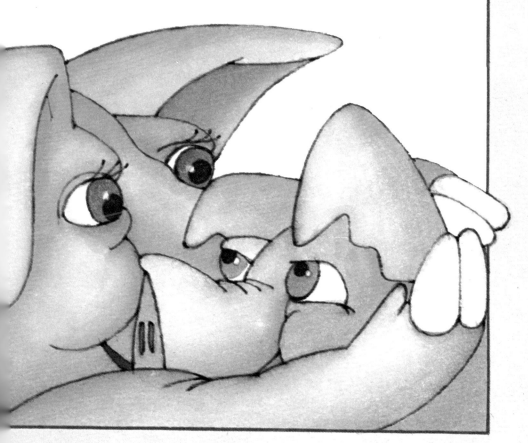

Quentin felt silly because he had forgotten. But he was so very hungry that he didn't feel silly for very long. He sat right down and ate a big dinner of corn.

After that he played tag with his brothers.

Then Quentin, his mother, and his brothers all lay down in the cool mud and took a nap.

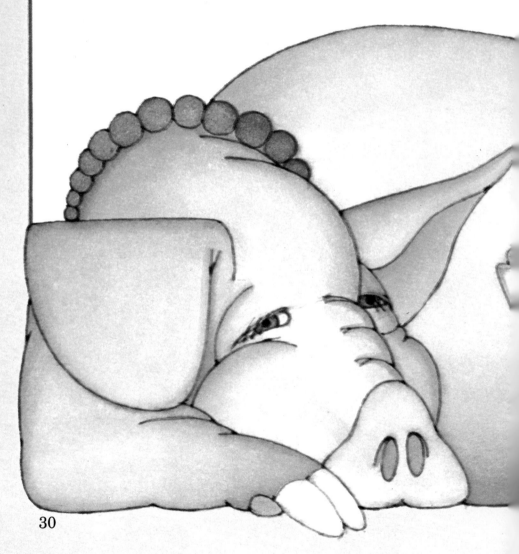

31

Jean Zelasney is a free-lance writer and the mother of two young sons.

In addition to giving practice with words that most children will recognize, *Do Pigs Sit in Trees?* uses the 39 enrichment words listed below.

bugs	farmer's	missing	scared
	farmhouse	mud	smart
check	felt		swim(ming)
chicks	field	nap	
cool	forgotten	nest(s)	tag
corn			tear
cornfield	ground	path	tired
		plenty	tracked
deep	hug	pond	tractor
dig(s)	hungry		
dirt		robin	wife
	idea	rolled	wonder
easy			
even			